The Transmogrification of Roscoe Wizzle

The Transmogrification
of
Roscoe Wizzle

David Elliott

SCHOLASTIC INC.
New York   Toronto   London   Auckland   Sydney
Mexico City   New Delhi   Hong Kong   Buenos Aires

ISBN 0-439-40594-7

Published by Scholastic Inc., 557 Broadway, New York, NY 10012,
by arrangement with Candlewick Press.
SCHOLASTIC and associated logos are trademarks
and/or registered trademarks of Scholastic Inc.

12 11 10 9 8 7 6 5 4 3 2   2 3 4 5 6 7/0

Printed in the U.S.A.   40

First Scholastic printing, April 2002
This book was typeset in Berling and Futura.

To Eli, for whom I would willingly transmogrify
—D. E.

Chapter 1

KINCHY SAYS that there is only one place to start. I told her that it was easy for her because she wasn't the one writing all this down, but she said I was just being a baby.

My name is Roscoe Wizzle. I am ten years old. I live with my parents in a pink house on Pleasant Street. It's kind of embarrassing for a ten-year-old boy to live in a pink house, but my parents don't seem to mind. In fact, they don't seem to mind much of anything.

My father, Waldo Wizzle, works in a cymbal factory. It's his job to make sure that the cymbals are loud enough when you crash them. All day long he bangs cymbals together and decides if they're loud enough. His nerves are shot. Sometimes when he comes home from work, he takes two giant wads of cotton and sticks them in his ears.

My mother, Wilma Wizzle, is an orphan. She was raised by a woman named Edna Edge at the Roseville Home for Lost Children. My mother says that Edna Edge is Roseville's biggest thorn. She has plenty of stories to tell about Miss Edge and her nephew, Sherman. Like the time it was Christmas and Edna Edge gave Sherman a brand-new red bicycle with a bell and everything. For *their* Christmas presents, each of the orphans was allowed to listen to Sherman ring the bell one time. I guess it's not easy being an orphan. Anyway, that's what my mother says.

My best friend is Kinshasa Rosa Parks Boomer.

Most people just call her Kinchy. You might think it's kind of strange for a ten-year-old boy to have a girl named Kinchy for his best friend, but there is nobody in this whole wide world like Kinchy Boomer. Absolutely nobody, and if you knew her, you would want her for a best friend, too. For one thing she has seen a lion. And not in a zoo, either.

Kinchy has been my neighbor since we were both three years old, and we know almost everything there is to know about each other. For example, I know that Kinchy is afraid that a black widow spider will get into her bed and bite her on the ankle, and she knows that I'm afraid that a comet will strike the earth when I am in the bathtub.

Kinchy was born in Africa, and as I said before, she has actually seen a lion. That's because her mother is an an-thro-pol-o-gist.

(I wrote it out like that because it has a lot of letters and sometimes I forget one if I'm not careful.) Kinchy says that an anthropologist is somebody who finds out stuff about other people, but not like a detective. Like they go to a village in Africa and study what everybody eats and what they like to do on their birthdays and what they believe about God and stuff like that.

To me, an anthropologist just sounds like someone who is nosy, but Kinchy says being an anthropologist is very interesting. Anyway, Kinchy's mother is an anthropologist and that's why Kinchy has seen a lion.

Oh, there's one other thing about Kinchy. She is a certified genius. She even speaks Swahili, which is the language they speak in the village in Africa where she saw the lion.

What else?

I go to Roseville Elementary School. I'm in

the fourth grade. My teacher's name is Mr. Bernard W. Pinchbeck.

I know his whole name because last year, when I was in the third grade, I found his wallet on the playground. When I opened it up to see who it belonged to, there was his driver's license with a picture and everything right there for anybody to see. That's when I found out his whole name—Bernard W. Pinchbeck. I also found out that he used to have bright red hair. Now he doesn't have any hair at all.

I don't know why Mr. Pinchbeck decided to be a teacher, since most of the time he acts like he doesn't even like kids. The only kid he's kind of nice to is Kinchy, and I think that's because he's afraid that she is smarter than he is, which she is. Whenever any of the kids have trouble with a math problem or spelling or anything at all, they go to Kinchy instead of B. W. Pinchbeck. I guess that *would* kind of drive you crazy. I don't know what the *W* stands for.

I'm writing all this down because Kinchy says that if I'm going to tell what happened, there are some things that you should know first, like who I am and where I live and stuff like that. (I wrote about B. Pinchbeck because it was kind of exciting and weird all at the same time to find his wallet. By the way, I forgot to tell you that he didn't give me a reward, even though it looked like there was plenty of money in his wallet. I didn't expect a reward or anything. I mean, I was just returning something that I found, but he didn't even *offer* me one. When I am a grownup I'm always going to offer a reward to any kid who finds something that I lost.)

Anyway, Kinchy says it's important to write all this stuff down because if I do and other kids read it, then what happened to me won't happen to them. And believe me, I wouldn't wish what happened to me on anybody, even though it's over now and I got through it and everything.

In a way, when you think about it, I guess it's good that it was *me*, and not somebody else, because now I'm okay and maybe another kid wouldn't have been. It's weird when you think about the kinds of things that happen to you and not to somebody else. Good things *and* bad things. In a way, it all kind of makes sense.

Anyway, I hope what happened to me never ever happens to anybody else. Nobody should ever have the awful, terrible, worst-ever experience of turning into a bug—not even Mr. Bernard W. Pinchbeck!

Chapter 2

I USED TO BE a normal kid. I mean, don't get me wrong, I still *am* normal. But once you get changed into a bug, you do see things a little bit differently even after your eyes get back to normal and everything. Anyway, a year ago I was probably just about like you. I went to school, did my homework, watched TV, and hung around with my best friend.

That was all before Gussy's came to town. Every kid in Roseville was wondering when we were going to get a Gussy's, since it seemed like almost every town in the whole world had one.

Then finally one day the sign appeared. COMING SOON! GUSSY'S! The sign was cool because there was a big picture of Gussy Gorilla on it, eating a Jungle Drum. Jungle Drums are Gussy's specialty. They're just about the biggest hamburgers in the world, with all kinds of special cheeses and sauces. I guess they're called Jungle Drums to go along with the way Gussy's restaurants are decorated inside with fake palm trees and stuff like that. It's cool!

I was more excited about the new Gussy's than most of the kids because it was only six blocks from my house.

Kinchy didn't care at all. She said she didn't see what the big fuss was about, but I think she was a little jealous because she's a vegetarian and she felt kind of left out. I told her to write to Gussy's to tell them to make a Jungle Drum for vegetarians. I even thought of a name for it—the

Jungle Veggie Wonderburger—but Kinchy said she couldn't be bothered. I still think it's a good name, though, and if I ever have a restaurant (which I probably won't), I'm going to put the Jungle Veggie Wonderburger on the menu.

But it wasn't only the kids who were happy about the new Gussy's. The grownups were excited, too, partly, I guess, because it was going to be built in an empty lot that every adult in Roseville said was an eyesore. For a long time people used to throw all kinds of trash in that lot, like old cans of paint and bug spray and stuff like that, but then they weren't allowed to do it any longer, so they stopped, most of them.

People told all kinds of stories about that lot. Some people said that if a bee from that lot stung you, your arm would swell up like a tomato, or that if you picked any of the wildflowers that grew there, you would have allergies for the rest of your life, even if you had never had them before. Butch Bigelow swears that his cat went in there to hunt mice and came out completely bald, which made me wonder if Bernard W. Pinchbeck had gone into that lot.

I never saw that cat, but Susu Johnson did. It scared her so bad that her mother called up Butch's mother and asked what was wrong with her, anyway, keeping a freaky cat like that around.

So, the sign announcing the new Gussy's went up in that lot, and before you knew it, there was a brand-new Gussy's Restaurant serving Jungle Drums faster than you could say Gussy Gorilla.

There was more excitement about Gussy's, too, because about three months before the restaurant opened, an article appeared in the *Roseville Recorder* that said Mr. Cecil Geed, owner and president of Gussy's International, was moving the Gussy's corporate headquarters to Roseville!

That was just about the biggest news that had hit Roseville since the time the tornado came to town and picked up an old lady, rocking chair and all. It put her down in the middle of a freeway miles and miles away. She didn't even know it, either. She just kept saying that she hadn't realized there was so much traffic on her street.

Cecil Geed was a zillionaire, and to have him move the Gussy's corporate headquarters to our town was a really big deal. His picture was in the paper almost every day. Sometimes he was with the mayor, sometimes he was by himself, and sometimes he was with his right-hand man, Willie Willies.

There was even a special article about Cecil Geed's secretary, Agnes Bean, who was seventy-three and a half years old and had just gotten her black belt in jujitsu. The article said that Agnes Bean's dream was to go on safari in Africa and that she studied jujitsu to protect herself from poachers.

I remember that article because my mother read it out loud when we were eating dinner.

"I'd like to meet that Agnes Bean," my mother said. "I wonder if she was an orphan."

"What's that?" my father asked.

He'd had a very bad day testing cymbals and had even more cotton in his ears than usual.

"She said she wonders if Agnes Bean was *an orphan*!" I shouted.

"No!" my father replied. "You definitely cannot have *a dolphin*! Why would a nice boy like you want a dolphin? Dolphins are a lot of trouble, and my nerves are shot as it is."

Chapter 3

I GUESS the trouble really began about three weeks after the new Gussy's opened. My father came home from testing cymbals, ran to the bathroom, and shoved some cotton in his ears. "What a day!" he said. "My nerves are shot."

"I'm sorry to hear that, dear," my mother said. "I know that you work very hard testing cymbals, but don't forget, it's not easy being an orphan, either."

I know that's what they said, because that's what they said every day. What was different this time was what happened next.

My mother and father used to take turns cooking dinner. One night, my mother; the next night, my father. To tell you the truth, neither of them is a very good cook. My father almost always made mashed potatoes because, according to him, they are a quiet, sensible food. He couldn't stand to have anything that crackled or crunched or made any kind of noise at all when you ate it.

When it was *her* turn, my mother usually made tuna surprise casserole. She made it so much because she liked the name.

"Tuna surprise is such a *cheerful* dish," she would say. "When I was an orphan, I never got any kind of surprise at all."

So meals at our house were kind of weird. One night it would be mashed potatoes, the next night, tuna surprise. The thing is, I would never have known they were weird if it hadn't been for

Kinchy. That's one thing that I found out. I mean, I used to think that everybody had mashed potatoes and tuna surprises all the time.

"I don't know how you stand it," Kinchy finally said.

Kinchy usually didn't say anything about my parents because (1) she is very polite and wouldn't want to hurt my feelings, and (2) her mother is an anthropologist and—according to Kinchy, who wants to be an anthropologist when she grows up—it's really bad for anthropologists to criticize other people.

But I guess sometimes she couldn't help herself.

"I mean, I know I'm a vegetarian junior anthropologist and everything," she would say, "but the food my mother makes at least tastes good. And she doesn't make the same thing every night, either."

I knew that was true because I ate at Kinchy's house sometimes, especially when her mother made couscous, which is delicious. It's like little tiny pasta things with vegetables over them. I guess it doesn't sound that good when you write it down, but it is, especially to someone who has eaten a lot of mashed potatoes and tuna surprises. If you ever get the chance to have couscous, you should try it. Another thing about couscous is that if you want to, you can scoop it up with your fingers instead of using a spoon, which sounds kind of gross but isn't. You just have to wash your hands first, that's all.

Anyway, on this particular night it was my father's turn to make dinner, but instead of making mashed potatoes, he asked me how would I like to ride my bike down to the new Gussy's and have a Jungle Drum for dinner. He said his nerves were too shot to cook.

Naturally, I said yes. What kid wouldn't? So he gave me the money and I rode my bike down to the new Gussy's. I was lucky not only because I was going to have a Jungle Drum for dinner but also because when I turned the corner where the Gussy's was, Gussy Gorilla himself was standing right there! It wasn't a real gorilla or anything, just somebody dressed up in a gorilla suit, but he looked real and that was cool.

I ordered a Jungle Drum Meal, which comes with Jungle Fries and a Quicksand, which is kind of like a milk shake without the milk or ice cream. I also got a Gussy Trading Card. All Jungle Drums come with Gussy Trading Cards, which are pictures of Gussy Gorilla doing all kinds of crazy things. They change the cards all the time, and kids collect those cards and trade them.

My Gussy Trading Card showed Gussy standing on a big painted ball. Later when I looked at it, I realized that it wasn't just any painted ball; it was a globe of the world. I guess I couldn't tell it was a globe at first because one of Gussy's feet was covering North America and the other one was covering Europe and part of Africa. When Kinchy saw my Gussy Trading Card she said that it looked like the globe was getting kind of squished, but I said maybe it was supposed to look like that.

Anyway, that night I ate my first Jungle Drum Meal and thought it was just about the most delicious thing I had ever eaten. I put my Gussy Trading Card on my wall with a piece of tape.

My mother didn't mind that my dad didn't make mashed potatoes that night because that meant she didn't have to do any dishes. Like I said, my parents took turns cooking, but whoever wasn't cooking had to do the dishes. Of course, there aren't that many dishes when you make mashed potatoes, especially when you make them the way my father did, with instant mashed potatoes that pour right out of a box. But still, my mom liked the idea because she had been very busy that day.

"Orphans get tired just like everybody else," she said.

In fact, my mother liked the idea so much that the next night, when it was her turn to cook, instead of making tuna surprise, *she* gave me money and I rode my bike down to the new Gussy's and had another Jungle Drum Meal. Of course, my father liked this because now *he* didn't have to do any dishes, which there are a lot of when you make tuna surprise.

This went on for a week, and then two weeks, and then finally it turned out that every night I was riding my bike down to the new Gussy's and ordering a Jungle Drum. I don't know what my parents ate on those nights. They never told me.

Sometimes, though, I would see two cereal bowls in the sink, with a little bit of milk left in the bottoms.

I thought I was the luckiest kid in the world. I was used to eating the same thing every other night anyway, and it was kind of nice to have a change from all those mashed potatoes and tuna surprises. But Kinchy said no kid on Earth should be eating Jungle Drums night after night for six months! She said it was downright dangerous!

As usual, she was right.

Chapter 4

IF YOU THINK about it, time is kind of weird. I mean, one day comes and you get up and brush your teeth and eat your breakfast and go to school (unless it's Saturday or something) and so on. And then the next day comes and the same thing happens and all those days seem pretty much the same.

I mean, I know there are little differences, like one day you might have a spelling test and another day you might have a geography test, but still, unless something really exciting happens (like a comet hitting the earth), which it almost never does, every day seems pretty much the same as the day before.

You get up in the morning and you look in the mirror and you think, *There I am. That's me, all right*. And you don't think about it anymore.

The weird thing is that certain things are happening all the time that you don't even know about. Like every day you could be getting just a tiny bit taller. A *really* tiny bit taller. Maybe only a *hair's width* taller! But still, if every day you add a hair's width, pretty soon, when you put on your jeans—the very same jeans that you've worn almost every day—suddenly, they're too short. They stop way above your ankles. But right until that very minute, you didn't even know it. You didn't look in the mirror every day and say, "Oh, I see I'm taller by the width of one hair." But the thing is, you *were*! That's the kind of thing I'm talking about.

And that's the kind of thing that happened to me. Only I wasn't getting taller. It was something else. Something horrible was happening to me. I didn't even know it, either. I was just getting up in the morning and saying, "Yep! That's me all right!" But the thing is, it wasn't! And the weird thing is if it hadn't been for Bernard W. Pinchbeck, I might not have found out until it was too late.

Every Friday Mr. Pinchbeck gives us a spelling test. The words aren't too hard, or anything—I mean, usually they are words like *brother* or *sister* or *father* or *mother*. Or something like that. Most kids can spell them without any trouble at all. But B. Pinchbeck always gives a bonus word, too, and those bonus words aren't easy. In fact, he usually picks words that no kid *or* grownup has heard of.

But mostly what he tries to do is pick words that Kinchy has never heard of. I don't get it. I mean, teachers are supposed to like it if a kid is smart, but that isn't the case with Mr. Bernard W. Pinchbeck when it comes to Kinchy Boomer. It drives him crazy that she is so smart, and so he always picks bonus words that are really weird just to show her that she isn't. And the other thing is that you don't just have to spell those bonus words. You also have to know what they mean.

It didn't take Kinchy long to figure out what was happening, so for her part, Kinchy began giving Mr. Pinchbeck a word *he* had never heard of. Of course, she didn't give him a test or anything like that. How could she? She is a kid and he is the teacher. But like I said, Kinchy is a certified genius. So every Friday she went out of her way to ask him a question with a word in it that she was sure *he* wouldn't know.

For example, she would say, "I certainly hope

this weekend won't be *lugubrious*. What do *you* think, Mr. Pinchbeck? Do you want the weekend to be *lugubrious*?"

Then B. W. Pinchbeck would do what he always did. He would start messing around with the papers on his desk and pretend like he was really busy, even though the second before that he hadn't been doing a thing. Then he would say something like, "What? Oh, I'm sorry, Kinshasa." (He never calls her Kinchy.) "Oh, I'm sorry, Kinshasa," he would say. "I didn't hear you. As you can see, I'm very busy right now. Ask me again after lunch."

Of course, at lunchtime what he would do is run straight to the library and look the word up so that he could answer Kinchy when she asked him again. The thing is, she never would ask him a second time. Sometimes he would even say things like, "What was that question you asked me this morning, Kinshasa? I have time to answer it now." But Kinchy would say something like, "I forget," or, "Oh, it wasn't really important."

In a way it was kind of embarrassing to see Mr. Pinchbeck hanging around waiting for Kinchy to ask him again, him being a grownup and everything. Sometimes I almost felt sorry for him. But as Kinchy always reminds me, *he* started it.

By the way, *lugubrious* means "gloomy." (Kinchy told me that.)

Anyway, on this particular Friday, after I had been going to Gussy's every night for about six months, Mr. Pinchbeck stood at the front of the room and looked straight at Kinchy the way he always did and said, "Today's bonus word is *transmogrify*. Does anybody know what *transmogrify* means?"

As it turned out on that Friday, Kinchy did know the meaning of that word (she knows them about half the time), so she raised her hand. At first B. Pinchbeck pretended like he didn't see her (he always does that), but finally he had to call on her.

"Yes, Kinshasa?" he said, looking at the ceiling. Mr. Pinchbeck has a habit of looking at the ceiling. "I suppose *you* know the meaning of *transmogrify*."

"Yes, I do, Mr. Pinchbeck," said Kinchy. "It means 'to change or transform, especially into something funny or comical.'"

"That is correct," Mr. Pinchbeck said, grinding his teeth (another bad habit). "*To transmogrify* means 'to change or transform, especially into something funny or comical.'"

That's when Susu Johnson did it. That's when she made me realize that my jeans stopped above my ankles, if you know what I mean.

"Like Roscoe Wizzle?" she said.

"Like Roscoe?" Mr. Pinchbeck asked. "What do you mean, Susu?"

"Well," she said, "Roscoe used to look like a regular kid, but now he looks funny."

"Susu!" said B. W. Pinchbeck. "Apologize to Roscoe! You shouldn't say such a thing to his face . . . even if it's true!"

"I'm sorry, Roscoe," said Susu. "But it *is* true. You look like you're changing into some kind of bug or something. Everybody thinks so. You're . . . you're *transmogrifying*!"

Chapter 5

NATURALLY, after school I ran home and looked into a mirror to see if what Susu said was true. I didn't even wait for Kinchy. I was too embarrassed. The horrible thing is that I found out it *was* true! When I looked in the mirror, I did look really weird! Mostly it was my eyes. They were huge and they looked like they were trying to pop right out of my head.

But it wasn't *just* my eyes. The shape of my face had changed, too. The last time I'd looked, it had been shaped like everybody else's face, sort of egg shaped. But now it was shaped more like an upside-down triangle, really wide at the top where my forehead was and really pointy and narrow down by my chin. I looked creepy! What Susu said was true! I looked like some kind of bug! I was *transmogrified*!

I know it seems kind of weird that I was changing into a bug and didn't even know it. So far, I have been able to think of three reasons why. Here they are:

1. I don't spend that much time looking into a mirror. Why should I? I am only ten years old.

2. Until Susu Johnson blurted it out right in front of everybody, nobody had told me. I mean, it seems like one of the ways you find out things about yourself is that somebody tells you. Like they

might say, "Your hair is sticking up," and then you go get some water and stick your hair down. But here's what I found out. When your hair is sticking up or something little like that, then almost anybody — even a total and complete stranger — will tell you. But when it's something big, like if you're changing into a bug, then almost nobody will tell you. I don't know why.

Later Kinchy told me that of course she had noticed that I was looking really weird but that she was waiting for just the right moment to say something about it. And anyway, she'd asked her mother and her mother had said it was probably just *a phase*. (That kind of makes me not trust anthropologists because there I was, changing into a bug, and her mother, a big anthropologist, said it was just a phase.)

I don't know why my parents, Waldo and Wilma, didn't notice. They thought it was just a phase, too, I guess. Anyway, at that time, my mother was very busy trying to get the Roseville Home for Lost Children reopened. It had been closed for many years and was nothing but a rundown building on the edge of town. She didn't want to open it as an orphanage but as a museum — an orphan's museum. She had even called Agnes Bean, Cecil Geed's personal secretary, to see if the owner and president of Gussy's International wanted to make a donation, which he didn't.

As for my father, well, his nerves were probably too shot to notice.

3. I was *preoccupied*. That means that I was always thinking about one certain thing and not noticing certain other things (like the fact that I was changing into a bug). This is probably the biggest reason that I didn't notice that I was changing into a bug. (I learned that word preoccupied from Kinchy, which is another reason that it's fun being her best friend—you learn a lot of stuff.)

I wasn't the only one who was preoccupied, either. Almost everybody in the whole town was (which is maybe another reason why nobody told me that I was changing into a you-know-what). Something was happening in Roseville. Something terrible! Almost the most terrible thing you could think of, and it was all anybody talked about.

Kids were disappearing!

So far, three kids had disappeared and no-body, including the chief of police, had a single clue about where they had gone. Some people said that they had just run away and that in *their* day when kids ran away, they got what was com-ing to them. Some said one thing, others said another, but nobody *really* knew where those kids were.

Butch Bigelow said he believed it was aliens—that aliens were coming to Roseville and snatching those kids and that the kids were probably in a human zoo somewhere on Mars right now.

Even though I kind of believe in aliens, I knew that Butch wasn't right because whoever had taken those kids always left a note. I didn't think aliens would leave a note—how would they know English?—and even if they did leave a note, it wouldn't be made of a lot of cutout let-ters from newspapers and magazines and then copied on a copier. Aliens could do a lot better than that. Here is what the note said:

Dear Parents of _____ :
We know you are worried about _____ , and we are sorry. We really are. But don't worry. He/she is fine. We will return him/her good as new just as soon as things are back to normal. Sincerely,

_____

(We can't tell you our names because we'd be in big trouble.)

In every case the note was the same, with the blanks filled out with the kid's name and *he* and *him* circled if it was a boy and *she* and *her* circled if it was a girl.

I guess those notes made the parents feel a little bit better, but they were still upset, because the note didn't say *when* things would get back to normal, and what was that supposed to mean, anyway?

The *really* creepy thing was that when you make a note with blanks and places to circle *he* or *she* and *him* or *her*, it means that you are going to need a lot of those notes — and that's what everybody was talking and wondering about.

Who was going to be next?

Anyway, that is probably the biggest reason that I didn't notice that I was changing into a bug until Susu Johnson said it in front of my whole class. In a way, I'm kind of glad she did. Who knows? If she hadn't, and Kinchy hadn't helped me, I might have even ended up with a full set of antennae like one of the other kids did.

Chapter 6

THAT NIGHT, Kinchy came over carrying her briefcase. To tell you the truth, I was kind of mad at her because she hadn't told me how weird I looked, and because of that, Susu Johnson had blurted it out right in front of everybody, and Susu isn't even my best friend! But it's hard to stay mad at Kinchy for long. Anyway, she came over with her briefcase, which meant that something serious was up even though I couldn't think of anything more serious than the way I looked.

Kinchy was doing her own investigation of the missing kids, only she called it *conducting*. She said she was *conducting* her own investigation, and she kept all the evidence in her briefcase. She had all the newspaper articles that had been written and copies of the notes and things like that.

She had other stuff, too, because believe it or not, her mother was helping the police investigate the case! According to Kinchy, if there is a really serious crime, like kids disappearing or something like that, the police hire all kinds of people to help them figure out what is happening — and one kind of person that they hire sometimes is an anthropologist. I guess it's because anthropologists know a lot about all different kinds of people, so they can look at clues and things and guess what kind of person is committing the crime. Anyway, Kinchy's mother was helping the police, and because of that, Kinchy knew all kinds of things that the rest of us didn't know.

To tell you the truth, I didn't exactly feel like

talking about those disappearing kids, even though I'd been preoccupied with them, because now I was preoccupied with something else— the fact that I was transmogrifying! I mean, I felt sorry for those kids and all, but not half as sorry as I was feeling for myself.

But it wasn't just that. I was scared!

I don't know if you've ever been *really* scared in your life. I hope not. I'm not talking about the regular kind of feeling scared, like when you see a scary movie, or about the kind of feeling scared when you know you did something that you shouldn't have and your parents haven't found it out yet. I'm talking about a different kind of feeling scared.

I don't know how to explain it. When I'm feeling a regular kind of feeling scared, it's like the fear is shooting right out of my fingertips; it's an emptying kind of feeling. But the *other* kind of feeling scared—the kind I'm talking about right now — is exactly the opposite. It's like fear is shooting *into* your fingertips, traveling right up your arms and into your brain and chest, filling you up with it. That's how I felt when Kinchy came over with her briefcase, like fear was shooting into my fingertips and filling me up so that nothing would be left, only the fear.

Before I had a chance to tell any of this to Kinchy or even tell her how mad I was at her, she grabbed me by the sleeve and pulled me back into the family room, which is a little room with a TV at the back of our house. It's kind of weird that we call it a family room, because we're never in there together, as a family, I mean. It's usually just me and the TV.

"Don't say a word," Kinchy said. "Do not say a single word."

She opened her briefcase and pulled out three pictures that had been cut out from the *Roseville Recorder*. She lined these up in a row on the coffee table. "Do you recognize these pictures?" she asked.

"Of course," I said. Anybody from Roseville would have recognized them. "Those are pictures of the three kids who disappeared. But listen, Kinchy, I—"

"Just answer the questions, please," Kinchy said. "Just answer the questions."

Even though Kinchy is my best friend, I have to admit that she is a little bit bossy sometimes. Besides, at this particular moment she was acting like she didn't care what Susu had said or how I might be feeling about it. She was acting really serious, like the only thing that *was* important was what *she* had to say.

"And do you know when these pictures were taken?" she asked. The way she was acting, I felt like I was some kind of suspect on a TV show or something.

"Of course I don't!" I said. "And what's more, I don't care! And by the way, Kinchy—"

"Those pictures . . . ," she said, interrupting me as if I hadn't even been talking, "were taken from one year to six months *before* the kids disappeared."

"Big whoop!" I said.

"This isn't the time for sarcasm," she said, just the way a grownup would.

She was making me really mad, especially because I wasn't sure what *sarcasm* meant. (As it turns out, it ended up being one of the bonus words that you-know-who gives. It means to *say* one thing but *mean* something else, like when you have a new pair of sneakers and someone says, "Oh, I *really* like your new sneakers," but you can tell by the way they're saying it, they actually think your new sneakers are stupid. That's what sarcasm is.)

Kinchy reached into her briefcase and pulled out three other pictures. I could tell by the paper they were printed on that these pictures hadn't come from the newspaper. One of them looked like it had been taken by those photographers who come around to your school. The other two were more like family snapshots or something.

"What I am about to show you," Kinchy whispered, "is *top secret*. You cannot tell a single soul about it, especially my mother because she doesn't know that I borrowed them. Under normal circumstances I would never have taken them. But things aren't normal. I think you'd better sit down before you see these."

Normally your best friend is supposed to make you feel better, but right then Kinchy Boomer was scaring me almost to death. Fear was shooting into my fingertips, the top of my head, my eyes. I didn't say a word. I couldn't. I just sat down and waited.

Kinchy put the pictures down on the coffee table.

"These are the *same* three kids," she said, "except these pictures are much more recent. The kids' parents gave them to the police, and the police gave them to my mom."

When I looked down at the pictures, I almost shouted, and I think I did make a weird kind of buzzing noise the way a hornet might. Those pictures didn't look at all like the pictures that had been printed in the newspaper. In fact, you could hardly tell that they were the same kids.

In the pictures that had been printed in the newspaper, the kids looked like any other kids. But in the pictures that were lined up on the coffee table, all three of the kids had huge eyes, eyes that looked like they were going to pop right out of their heads. And all three of their faces were shaped like upside-down triangles.

"They . . . they've been transmogrified!" I said.

"Right," Kinchy said. "And it can only mean one thing."

"Wh . . . what?" I stammered.

"You're next!" she said looking me straight in the eyes. "You're going to be the next kid to disappear!"

Chapter 7

KINCHY PUT the three pictures back into her brief-case, which was good because I couldn't stand to look at them any longer. Would you have wanted to? I mean, let's say that you were turning into a dog or something, and your best friend showed you pictures of three other kids who looked like *they* were turning into dogs — like maybe they had pointed noses and they were really hairy and their tongues were hanging out of their mouths. Would you have wanted to look at those pictures? I'll bet you wouldn't have, especially if those kids had disappeared and you thought you were going to be next.

"There must be some connection between those three kids and you," Kinchy said. "There *has* to be!"

"Of course there's a connection," I said. "We all look like praying mantises!"

"That's not what I mean," she said. "I mean *before* you were transmogrified. You must have been connected somehow before you all changed. And look, here's something else. You have to stop feeling sorry for yourself. I'm sure it isn't easy to discover that you are metamorphosing into a bug." (That's the exact word she used, too — *metamorphosing* — which is a fancy word for changing.) "I'm sure it must be very hard. But feeling sorry for yourself isn't going to change anything. Right now, if I'm going to solve this, I need your help. You need to think!"

That's one thing about Kinchy. She doesn't mess around. In a way, it's helpful.

She took out the three newspaper pictures and put them back on the coffee table.

"Now look at these," she said. "'Do you recognize any of these kids? Think, Roscoe, *think*!"

It gave me a really funny feeling when Kinchy asked me if I recognized those kids, because when each of the pictures first appeared in the *Roseville Recorder*, I thought I *had* recognized them even though I'd never *met* them. They didn't go to Roseville Elementary. The *Roseville Recorder* said that two of them were home-schoolers and the other one went to a private school, the Academy for the Extremely Right-Brained Child, or something like that. Anyway, every time a kid disappeared, they put the kid's picture in the paper, and every time, I thought that the kid had looked familiar—like I knew them from somewhere. I never mentioned it to anybody, though, because:

1. The newspaper pictures weren't that good. They were kind of blurry and everything, so in a way, those kids might have been anybody.

2. I have a very active imagination. Everybody says so. Like one time I was in the bathtub and my mother had burned the tuna surprise, so the house got kind of filled with smoke and I thought that a comet really had hit the earth. So I thought I was probably just imagining that I knew those kids.

3. It was too dumb. I mean, why would I recognize kids who had disappeared?

4. It was too scary! It was scary enough that kids were disappearing, but it was

even scarier when you thought you knew them.

"Think!" said Kinchy again. "We may not have much time!"

I picked up the first picture. It was Charlie Bog—the first kid to disappear. Like I said, the picture wasn't too good, but you could still see Charlie Bog's face pretty clearly. The picture must have been taken at a birthday party or something because he was wearing one of those little pointed hats and eating a big piece of cake. OH WHERE, OH WHERE HAS MY LITTLE BOG GONE? was the caption under the picture.

I got the same feeling I did when I first saw that picture of Charlie—that I had seen him somewhere before. But even though I was trying as hard as I could, I couldn't think where. Every time I felt myself getting close to the answer, I could feel it dart off to another part of my brain or something.

It was like when you try to stick two magnets together but you have them backward, so instead of sticking together, they push each other apart. It was something like that, and it was driving me crazy.

The same thing happened with the other two pictures, too. I felt like my brain was going to explode.

Kinchy was being very patient, which she knew how to be because, according to her, anthropologists have to be patient. As she says, an African village isn't going to tell you everything about itself in one day. She just sat down and waited in the overstuffed chair that my mother bought because she said that when she was at the Home for Lost Children, Edna Edge always let her nephew, Sherman, sit in a big comfy chair but the orphans always had to sit on wooden stools.

I was sweating and looking at that picture of Charlie Bog for about the hundredth time when a Gussy's commercial came on TV. (The TV was always on in that room. I don't know why.) Anyway, I looked up and there was Gussy Gorilla peeking between the fake palm trees at Cecil Geed, owner and president of Gussy's International. Cecil Geed was sitting in a booth at Gussy's next to his right-hand man, Willie Willies, and both of them were grinning like they had just won a trip to somewhere they really wanted to go.

As Gussy sang the words to the Gussy's jingle, Geed and Willies beat on the table with their hands like they were drummers or something. I always thought it wasn't fair that Agnes Bean didn't get to be in it. After all, she *was* seventy-three and a half years old, and she *did* have her black belt in jujitsu.

I had seen that commercial before.

Gussy G. is prowling, prowling.

Boom da-da! Boom da-da! Boom! Boom! Boom!

Can't you hear his stomach growling?

Boom da-da! Boom da-da! Boom! Boom! Boom!

He's just an ape, but he's not dumb!

Boom da-da! Boom da-da! Boom! Boom! Boom!

He's searching for those Jungle Drums!

Special sauces!

Boom! Boom! Boom!

Special cheeses!

Bang! Bang! Bang!

Jungle Fries and Quicksand Freezes!

And a Gussy's Trading Card!

Eat at Gussy's! It's not hard!

Boom da-da! Boom da-da! Boom! Boom! Boom!

Boom da-da! Boom da-da! Bang! Bang! Bang!

Suddenly when I heard that last *Bang!* the answer was clear to me, just like I had turned one of those magnets around and the other one came snapping right into place. Maybe all the drumming that Cecil Geed and Willie Willies had done banged the answer right into my head.

"That's it!" I shouted. "That's where I have seen them! Gussy's!"

It all came back to me then. I had seen Charlie Bog and the other two kids almost every day at Gussy's. They were either ahead of me in the line, or behind me, or sometimes I saw them with their parents in the Gussy's drive-through.

I felt so good to finally figure that out. It is really weird to think that a person could feel good even when he was changing into a bug and thinks that note-leaving kidnappers might snatch him, but I did. I felt good.

"It was Gussy's!" I said again.

Kinchy sat there for a minute, not saying anything. I thought she would be happy that I had finally figured it out, but she didn't look happy. She looked like she was thinking.

"Can I use your phone?" she said at last. "Don't worry. It's a local call."

"I'm not worried," I said. "At least I'm not worried about that."

But I don't think she even heard me. She was already punching a number into the buttons on the phone. I could hear the beeps those buttons make. To me they always sound like the beginning of a little song. I could hear Kinchy talking, too, but I couldn't understand a thing she was saying. It was almost like she was talking in code or something.

She was on the phone for a couple of minutes. Then she hung up and walked back to me.

"What are you doing at five o'clock tomorrow morning?" she asked.

Chapter 8

AT FIVE O'CLOCK the next morning, Kinchy and I were walking down the street to Gussy's. I had left a note for my parents, saying that I was helping Kinchy do some anthropological work and I would be back soon.

I don't know if you've ever been up really early in the morning and walked through your neighborhood. If you have you know how different it is than at a regular time when everybody is awake and doing something like mowing the lawn or going to work or washing the car.

In a way it reminded me of being in school when the art teacher gives you a blank piece of paper. I know it sounds crazy, but I always think that once I draw a picture on the paper, it won't be blank anymore and that, instead, it will be a picture. I don't know why I think crazy things like that. I just do sometimes.

Anyway, that's the same kind of thing I was thinking when I was walking with Kinchy to Gussy's at five o'clock in the morning, when not a single soul was up and moving around except us. I was thinking, once we get to Gussy's, this day will never be the same as it is right now.

I wasn't even sure what we were going to do once we got to Gussy's. Kinchy hadn't told me. She had just said that we had to conduct a thorough investigation. And that we had to do it before anybody else was around.

"But how *can* it be thorough?" I'd asked. "Gussy's is closed."

Gussy's opened at 6:30 A.M. We wouldn't even be able to get inside, and once it was open, they weren't going to let us go snooping around.

"I've taken care of all that," was all Kinchy had said.

Right now, we weren't saying a word.

It wasn't dark, but it wasn't really light, either, and it made everything seem kind of not real. But as we turned the corner and I could see the Gussy's sitting where that weird empty lot used to be, my heart started beating so fast that I could feel it way up at the top of my throat.

Plus, now that I knew I was transmogrifying—that I was changing into some kind of bug—I could actually *feel* it happening. At least, I thought I could. I felt all twitchy and weird, and my eyes felt like they were spinning around in my head. It was awful.

When we got about a half block from Gussy's, I could see that someone was lurking around in front of the restaurant, someone really weird looking, kind of huge and hairy.

"Kinchy," I whispered, "do you see that? It's Gussy Gorilla! What's *he* doing here?"

But Kinchy kept right on walking. In fact, she sped up. That was just like her.

"Come on," she said. "I told you. I've taken care of everything."

So I followed her.

What difference does it make? I thought. *I'm turning into a bug.*

Kinchy walked right up to Gussy.

Then she said something really weird. It sounded like she said, "*Jambo,*" or something. And what was even weirder was that Gussy said the same thing.

"*Jambo,*" Kinchy said.

"*Jambo, toto,*" said Gussy.

I didn't even try to understand what was happening. Maybe this was what happened when you changed into a bug. Everything goes crazy.

Your best friend walks up to someone in a gorilla suit and says things like *jambo* and they understand her and say *jambo* back.

The other thing I thought was maybe this is what humans sound like to bugs. Like maybe what Kinchy had really said was, "Good morning," but to me it sounded like *jambo* because I was changing into a bug.

But then Gussy said, "Follow me," so I knew that I wasn't a complete bug yet, because at least I understood *that*, and I felt a lot better.

We walked around to the back of the restaurant.

"Roscoe," Kinchy said, "I'd like to introduce you to someone."

Gussy took off his head—I mean the gorilla head—and when he did—I mean, *she* did, because it was a woman—I couldn't believe it! It was an old lady!

"Roscoe," Kinchy said, "meet Cecil Geed's personal secretary, Agnes Bean!"

"*Jambo*, Roscoe!" said Agnes Bean.

Chapter 9

"YOU'RE GUSSY GORILLA?" I almost shouted. "Agnes Bean is Gussy Gorilla? But you're seventy-three and a half years old!"

"Cecil Geed makes me do it," said Agnes. "It's part of my job. And by the way, I'm seventy-four now. *Tempus fugit* and all that, you know."

"But how? . . ." I asked, looking at Kinchy.

I was so surprised that I couldn't even finish my question, but Kinchy understood me, anyway, which is one of the reasons it's great to have a best friend. "I am Agnes Bean's Swahili teacher," she said.

Remember that I told you that Agnes Bean's dream was to go on safari in Africa and she had gotten her black belt in jujitsu to protect herself from poachers? Well, as it turns out she wanted to be able to call for help in case she and a poacher got into a wrangle — that's what she called it, a wrangle — so when the Gussy's corporate headquarters moved to Roseville, Agnes had put an ad in the paper, advertising for a Swahili teacher because that's one of the languages they speak in Africa.

Kinchy had seen the ad. She reads the newspaper every day — all of it! — starting with the headlines and finishing with those little advertisements that are always in the back, which is where Agnes Bean had advertised. Anyway, since Kinchy is a certified genius and was born in Africa and speaks Swahili and everything, she called Agnes Bean.

Kinchy had been teaching Swahili to Miss Bean for almost six months! I couldn't believe she hadn't told me, but she said it was because it seemed a bit like bragging. Kinchy thought bragging was one of the worst things in the world, which was funny since she herself had so much to brag about—I mean, being a certified genius and everything. That's another thing I've noticed. The people who really have something to brag about almost never do, and the people who brag the most are the people who have nothing to brag about and are usually not telling the truth, anyway.

Agnes and Kinchy had hit it off immediately. Unlike a certain fourth-grade teacher, Agnes Bean appreciated how special Kinchy was.

When Kinchy realized that my getting turned into a bug and those three kids disappearing were somehow connected to Gussy's, she called Agnes.

And that's how the three of us—Kinchy

Boomer, certified genius and my best friend; me, Roscoe Wizzle, a normal kid who was changing into a bug; and Agnes Bean, Cecil Geed's personal secretary, with a black belt in jujitsu and dressed in a gorilla suit—got to be standing together behind Gussy's Restaurant at five o'clock in the morning. (By the way, *jambo* is how you say hello in Swahili.)

"I thought it wouldn't look so suspicious if I wore the Gussy costume," said Agnes, taking a set of keys out of a pocket.

"Gussy has pockets?" I said.

"For tissues and things," said Agnes. "You wouldn't believe how hot it gets under here. We'd better get started."

"But won't you get in trouble for letting us in?" I asked her. "Won't Cecil Geed get mad and fire you?"

"I hope he does!" said Agnes. "I have been his

personal secretary for over twenty-five years, and do you know how many raises he has given me? Not a single one! He says he can't afford it, but every year he buys himself a brand-new bright red sports car! And every year when he does, he says the same thing. 'I have a treat for you, Agnes,' he says, and do you know what that treat is? He drags me out to the street and makes me listen to him honk the horn of that car!

"I've scrimped and saved my whole life and finally have enough money to fulfill my dream. I'm retiring next week and going on safari at last! Poachers beware, and good riddance to Mr. Cecil Geed!"

She walked over to Gussy's back door, opened it, and we walked in, Agnes first, Kinchy second, and me last.

At first everything seemed kind of normal. It just looked like an empty Gussy's, but after a few seconds Kinchy kind of stiffened, like she had been turned into a statue or something.

She put her finger to her lips and motioned for us not to make a sound.

That's when I heard it, a kind of scuttling or scratching noise.

Kinchy remained still as a statue. Even in the dim light of the restaurant, I could see her thinking, pushing her eyebrows down and scrunching up her lips, trying to figure out what that sound was. Agnes Bean struck a jujitsu pose, and that didn't make me feel any better, either.

I was just standing there, trying not to make any noise but at the same time feeling like I wanted to shout. That's when I saw it. I think I was the first one to see it because my eyes had gotten so big and could take in more light than Kinchy's and Agnes's.

It was a bug! A huge bug, about the size of a platter that a really big Thanksgiving turkey would get served on! It was halfway up the side of a big machine. I guess that bug couldn't read, though, because in front of the machine was a sign with big red letters that said:

DANGER! KEEP AWAY! MEAT GRINDER!

At first I thought the bug was just a shadow or something, but then it moved in that creepy way bugs have of moving, waving their antennae around and everything, except that this bug's antennae were about two feet long, which made it *really* creepy.

I couldn't help it. I shouted, and in the same second that I did, Kinchy snapped on a flashlight just in time for all of us to see the bug drop right into the meat grinder.

"Roscoe!" Kinchy shouted. "You've been eating giant bugs!"

That's when Willie Willies popped up from

behind the counter like some kind of weird jack-in-the-box. He was holding a giant butterfly net, and that scared me almost as much as that bug did!

Cecil Geed popped up right next to Willies.

"Bean!" he shouted. "What are *you* doing here?"

"What am *I* doing here?" Agnes Bean shouted right back. "What are *you* doing here?"

"What do you think I'm doing?" he answered. "I'm trying to help Willies catch that giant bug that you just caused to fall into the meat grinder. A CEO doesn't get to be a CEO by sitting in his office all day, you know!"

"And how does he get to be CEO?" said Agnes Bean. "By serving innocent children sandwiches made of giant bugs?"

"Just for that," said Geed, "I'm never going to let you listen to me honk the horn of my brand-new red cars again!"

"Big whoop!" she shouted right back.

Then she let out some kind of weird jujitsu sound. I couldn't believe a seventy-four-year-old lady could make a sound like that, but she did.

"Get 'em, Willies!" Geed shouted as he ran for the back door. "Get all of 'em! But get that bug boy first!"

Chapter 10

CECIL GEED TOOK OFF toward the back door, with Agnes Bean shrieking like a samurai right behind him. I wasn't sure what had happened to Kinchy. I couldn't see her anywhere. Anyway, I didn't have much time to think about it because I suddenly found myself alone with Willie Willies.

You probably have never been chased around a restaurant with a jungle theme by a right-hand man holding a giant butterfly net. At least, I hope you haven't, because believe me, it's not fun, especially when you have just found out that you've been eating giant bugs and you are turning into a bug yourself.

I must have been in shock or something, because at first I just stood there. But suddenly Willie Willies hopped up on the counter and took his first swoop at me. I couldn't believe that he could hop like that. It was almost like he was some kind of bug himself. But he did hop. He hopped and swooped.

There are two things that I think I'll never forget, even though I want to, and one of them is the way Willie Willies hopped up onto the counter like that, with both legs at the same time. It makes me think that people can do almost anything.

The other thing that I think I'll never forget is the way that giant butterfly net sounded when it swooshed past my head. Now I always wonder if that's what butterflies hear when someone is trying to catch them. If it is, I feel really sorry for them, because it's not a nice sound. It's a really scary sound! I'm not even sure if butterflies have ears, but I kind of hope they don't, because I don't want them to hear that *swoosh*!

When Willie Willies hopped and swooped, I stopped thinking about the fact that I had been eating giant bugs, and instead realized that I had better get out of there. Willies took another swoop. He came really close to getting me, so I jumped backward, but when I did, I ran right into one of the fake palm trees. I hit it so hard that all the fake coconuts came bouncing down around my ears and onto the floor.

"Those fake palm trees aren't cheap, mister," Willies shouted from on top of the counter. "You break 'em, you bought 'em."

He hopped down from the counter and landed on one of the fake coconuts, which rolled out from under him and sent him sprawling onto the floor.

"Why you spiteful brat!" he shouted. "I could have hurt myself!"

74

I still don't know why Willie Willies thought *I* was spiteful, since *he* was the one trying to catch *me* in a giant butterfly net. But I knew this was my chance to get out of there, so I took off toward the door. I almost made it, too. My fingers were stretched out, ready to grab onto the handle, but then *I* stepped on one of those fake coconuts and went sliding across the floor and ran into another of those fake palm trees. More fake coconuts came raining down. It's a good thing those coconuts *were* fake, or I could have gotten a serious concussion or something.

I don't know how long Willie Willies and I ran around that restaurant, but it seemed like the whole time we did, fake coconuts were falling down on us. Every time you took a step, you stepped onto one of those coconuts, and when you did, you went sliding into another fake palm tree. At least, I did. For some reason Willie Willies never ran into a single tree. But the weird thing was that every time *I* did and more coconuts would come falling down, he would tell me that I was going to have to pay for them.

"*I'm* not paying for that!" he would shout. "*You* are! It's your fault. If you would just let me catch you in this giant butterfly net, you wouldn't have to be knocking all these fake coconuts onto the floor! Cecil Geed, owner and president of Gussy's International, will not be pleased."

"Well, I'm not pleased to be changing into a bug," I said right back.

"Oh, stop being such a baby," Willies said. "How many other kids get such an interesting opportunity?"

I wonder now if I couldn't have escaped by trying to climb one of the walls or by hopping up onto the ceiling or something. After all, I was changing into a bug, and bugs can walk on floors and ceilings. In fact, that's one of the things that make them bugs, but at the time, I didn't think of it. I'm really sorry now that I didn't. It would have been fun. The weird thing, though, is that sometimes I dream that I can do it. Not as a bug but as me. "Hi, everybody," I say in my dream. "It's me. It's Roscoe Wizzle and I'm walking on the ceiling."

Anyway, I didn't try it, and Willie Willies finally caught me in the giant butterfly net.

"I've been counting up those coconuts," he said. "You owe Cecil Geed, owner and president of Gussy's International, two hundred dollars and thirteen cents."

Then everything went dark.

Chapter 11

WHEN WILLIE WILLIES let me out of the giant bag he had thrown over me, I was in some kind of office in what looked like an abandoned building or something. The windows were all cracked and dirty, and there wasn't a rug on the floor, or anything that would make it look like somebody lived there. I said it was an office, because the top half of the door to the room was made of glass and there was some writing on it. I couldn't tell what it said because it was on the other side of the glass, so it looked backward from where I was inside the room.

Anyway, as it turned out, the building wasn't

that abandoned because Willie Willies and I weren't alone. There were other people in it, *three* other people. That's right! I was in a room with the three kids who had disappeared! It was a good thing that Kinchy had shown me those pictures, too, because otherwise I wouldn't have recognized them.

Charlie Bog had actually grown antennae!

"Oh, hello," he said. "I see that you're one of uz-z-z! How far along-ng-ng-ng are you? Getting-ng-ng your antennae yet?"

He was a little hard to understand because when he talked it was like half of his voice was *hum* and the other half was *buzz*. He and the other two kids were sitting on the floor playing Monopoly just like they were at home or something.

"Did you bring-ng-ng uz-z-z our breakfaz-z-t, Mr. Williez-z-z?" asked one of the other kids. I think it was Judy Pongarongatong, but I wasn't sure because they all looked so much alike, just like bugs do.

"Did you bring us our breakfast, Mr. Willies?" Willie Willies repeated, trying to make fun of Judy by making his voice sound that buzzing way. "Of course, I didn't. I didn't have time. What am I, anyway? Your personal secretary?"

"Well, you did kidnap us, you know," said the third kid, Polly Rickenbacker. "The least you could do is bring us our breakfast."

For some reason Polly was much easier to understand than Charlie or Judy.

"We kidnapped you for your own good, and you know it!" snapped Willie Willies. "You were turning into bugs, and we had to do something about it."

"That waz-z-z-n't for our own-n-n-n good," said Judy Pongarongatong. "It waz-z-z for *your* own-n-n-n good, yourz-z-z and that Cecil Geed, or whatever hiz-z-z-z name iz-z-z-z!"

"You leave Cecil Geed, owner and president of Gussy's International, out of it, missy!" Willies said. "Is it his fault if nobody would want to eat at a restaurant that's crawling with giant bugs?"

"Not *juz-z-zt* giant bugz-z-z," said Charlie Bog. "Giant bugz-z-z that fall into the meat grin-n-n-der and chan-n-n-nge whoever eatz-z-z them into bugz-z-z, too."

"Oh, so what?" barked Willies. "People are too fussy."

For a second nobody said anything. Charlie just twitched his antennae and Willie Willies fiddled with his giant butterfly net.

"If people find out about those bugs," Willies said all of a sudden, "Gussy's would close quicker than you could drop a Quicksand."

"But it *should* cloz-z-ze if it's changing kidz-z-z into bugz-z-z," Charlie Bog buzzed.

"That's *your* opinion," snapped Willies. "In *my* opinion, most kids would be improved if they changed into bugs. Anyway, it doesn't change all kids into bugs. Only *certain* kids. Certain kids who make little piggies of themselves."

Willies squinted his eyes and looked right at me when he said that.

"But I didn't make a piggy of myself," said Polly Rickenbacker. "I've never even been to Gussy's!"

"Yeah! Right!" said Willie Willies. "Tell me another one!"

"I haven't!" said Polly, and she stamped her foot the way people do when they're really mad and can't think of anything else to do. "I think it's a disgusting place with that gorilla running around everywhere!"

The way she said that and stamped her foot and everything made me think she was telling the truth.

"Well, I *did* make a piggy of myself," said Charlie Bog. "And I'm proud of it! I ate there seven-n-n-ty-seven-n-n-n dayz-z-z in-n-n a row!"

"I don't understand what the big fuss is about, anyway!" Willie Willies said. "How many times do I have to tell you? Dr. Tristan VanNutz from the I.S.G.B. said that in time the bug process will reverse itself. You won't be bugs forever."

One thing I have noticed is that really weird situations can seem really normal. I mean, here I was turning into a bug with three other kids who were turning into bugs and we had all been kidnapped, but somehow it didn't seem that bad. The other kids were playing Monopoly and everything, and they were talking to Willie Willies not like he was their friend or something but at least like someone they had gotten to know.

"What is that, anyway?" I asked. "That I.S.G.B.?"

"I can't believe what kids don't know these days," said Willie Willies. Then he clicked his tongue. "The I.S.G.B., mister, just happens to be the Institute for Science Gone Bad. It's in London, England. We called Dr. VanNutz there and told him what was happening, that every once in a while a giant bug would accidentally fall into the meat grinder and that if you ate at Gussy's often enough you were bound to get one mixed into your Jungle Drum."

"But where do those bugs come from?" I asked.

Willie Willies turned to me. "All restaurants have bugs!" he snapped. "Don't they teach you anything in that school you go to? Don't you take science?"

"But not all restaurants have *giant* bugs!" I said.

"You'd be surprised, mister!" Willies replied. "You'd be surprised."

"And even if they did," I continued, "they wouldn't turn you into a bug if you ate one."

"And how would you know about that, Dr.

Smarty Pants?" said Willies. "I suppose you've been eating bugs all your life! I suppose you're a professional bug-eater!"

I don't know why Willie Willies was so mad at me. One thing I've noticed is that there are certain people who when they're doing something really bad—like catching you in a giant butterfly net and kidnapping you—try to make you feel like *you're* doing something really bad even though you're not. Willie Willies was definitely that kind of person.

"Cut it out, Mr. Williez-z-z," said Charlie Bog. "And tell him about the lot."

"You be quiet about that lot!" Willies barked.

"What lot?" I asked.

"There is nothing wrong with that lot!" Willies practically shouted.

"Come on!" I said. "Somebody tell me. What lot?"

"An empty lot," said Polly Rickenbacker.

"An empty lot where for yearz-z-z and yearz-z-z people had been-n-n dumping all kin-n-nds of nasty thingz-z-z," said Judy Pongarongatong.

"An empty lot where those nasty thingz-z-z started mixing together to make new, even-n-n nastier thingz-z-z," said Charlie Bog.

Suddenly I understood. It was as clear to me as if someone had turned on a little light in a dark corner of my brain.

"A lot where those new nasty things started turning regular little bugs into bugs the size of turkeys!" I said.

"What a genius," I heard Willie Willies mutter.

"And a lot," I continued, "where the owner and president of Gussy's International built one of his restaurants even though he must have known about those bugs!"

I knew that he must have known because we had learned in a school project that before you can build anything like a house or a restaurant or an office building, engineers have to do all kinds of tests on the ground first.

"That lot was cheap!" barked Willie Willies. "If it didn't make giant bugs that turned kids who ate them into other giant bugs, it would have been perfect!"

Chapter 12

SO THAT WAS IT! We had been eating mutant bugs at Gussy's, and those mutant bugs were turning *us* into bugs! (I know that word *mutant* because I *do* take science in school, which I would have told Willie Willies if he had given me a chance.) And now I understood the mystery of that weird lot, too, and all the rumors people told about it.

One thing I have noticed is that you never really know what you're going to think or when you're going to think it. Like when I found out about that lot, it seems really weird but the first thing that popped into my head was Butch Bigelow's bald cat! I felt so sorry for that cat.

It probably never knew why it went bald.

The other thing that I wondered about was Polly Rickenbacker. She said she'd never eaten at Gussy's, and I believed her because of the way she stamped her foot and everything. So why was she changing into a bug? If Kinchy had been there, she probably would have been able to figure it out right away, but Kinchy wasn't there. And where was *there*, anyway?

"Where are we?" I asked.

Willie Willies turned to me again. The way he did that, all jerky and everything, reminded me of animals that I had seen on nature shows on TV, like when one of those antelopes knows it's going to get caught by a lion or something.

I know I was supposed to be mad at Willie Willies because, after all, he had chased me all around Gussy's with a giant butterfly net and had thrown a bag over me and brought me here and everything, but really I felt kind of sorry for him.

If Kinchy had been there I know what she would have said. *"Don't forget. He started it."* Anyway, I didn't feel that sorry.

"What do you mean, 'Where are we?'" he barked. "Didn't you read what was written on the door when we came in, you little ignoramus?"

"How could I read it?" I asked him. "I was in a bag!"

"I'll bet you drive your teacher crazy with excuses like that," he said.

"Well what *does* it say?" I asked.

"Read it for yourself," said Willies. "If you *can* read, that is."

He turned his back on me and walked over to Charlie Bog and told him to stop twitching his antennae. But Charlie said he couldn't help twitching his antennae and that they twitched all by themselves.

I walked over to the door.

Like I said before, you could see some writing that had been painted on the top half of the door, which was made of glass. There were three lines of words. The first line only had two words, and each word had four letters. I started with the second word because I knew that line was backward, so the second word was really the first word. (If you don't believe me, print your whole name on a piece of white paper and then turn the paper around and hold it up to the light. If you do, you'll find out that your last name is first!) The letters were backward, too, but if I concentrated really hard, I could make them out.

The first letter was *E*. The next one was *D*. It was followed by *N*. *EDN*. The last letter was *A*, which was easy because an *A* looks the same forward and backward. *EDNA*. *EDNA* was followed by another word with four letters, and the first letter of that word was an *E*, too. Just like in the

Chapter 13

SO FAR I HAVE discovered that there are at least five different kinds of minutes:

1. The Rubber Band

2. The Firecracker

3. The JAM

4. The Diamond

5. The Sleeping Beauty

There are probably a lot more, but like I said, so far I have only discovered five.

The Rubber Band is the longest minute there is. It can stretch out forever. Like if you're at the doctor's office waiting to get a shot.

The Firecracker is the opposite of the Rubber Band. Pretend that you've been waiting all day to open your birthday presents. Then you finally get to. You tear off the wrapping paper and open the boxes and see your presents. Suddenly it's all over. It was so short it seems like it exploded and was never there in the first place. That's why I call it the Firecracker.

The JAM, which stands for "Just a Minute," can be either really short or really long, because when people say they'll do something in "just a minute," you never know how long it will be. It could be one second, or it could be a whole hour.

The Diamond is very rare because it actually seems like sixty seconds, which is what a minute is supposed to be.

Remember when Sleeping Beauty pricks her finger and everybody suddenly goes to sleep, but years later, the Prince comes and everybody wakes right up just like nothing happened? Well, that's what I mean by the Sleeping Beauty, only it isn't years, it's just a minute, a minute that gets lost.

I'm telling you all this because when I read what was printed on that door and found out that I was turning into a bug in Edna Edge's office at the Roseville Home for Lost Children, I had a real Sleeping Beauty. But it was backward because it was like the rest of the world had gone to sleep and I was the only one there.

It's kind of hard to explain, and I haven't told this to anyone—not even Kinchy because it sounds too weird—and I'm afraid that nobody will believe me. But *I* know it happened, and I guess that's all that really matters. Anyway, after

I read what was written on the door, I just stood there, and like I said, it was like I was the only one there even though I knew I wasn't.

That's when I heard it.

I only heard it once, but the weird thing is I knew what it was right away. It was just about the saddest sound I have ever heard, too. It was a bicycle bell. I don't know where the sound of that bell came from. That's one of the reasons I haven't told anybody. They would probably say that it came from outside, or something like that. But I know it didn't, because I knew whose bicycle bell it was, echoing in that room after all those years. All of a sudden I knew that I was turning into a bug in the very room where my mother had stood years and years ago as a little girl on Christmas morning, listening to Edna Edge's nephew, Sherman, ring the bell on his brand-new red bicycle.

And I know it sounds strange, but I remember thinking, *I bet my mother can still hear the sound of that bell.* I bet she hears it all the time.

Chapter 14

THE NEXT THING I knew, Charlie Bog was asking me a question. "Do you wan-n-nt to play Mon-n-n-nopoly?" he asked.

I don't know how long I had been standing there when he asked me that, or even if he had asked me more than one time. That's the tricky part about the Sleeping Beauty. You never do know.

To tell you the truth, after I heard the sound of that bell, I didn't really feel like playing Monopoly. But there wasn't that much to do at the Roseville Home for Lost Children. Also,

I was trying to follow Kinchy's advice from the day before, which was to stop feeling sorry for myself, so I said that I would play. I sat down on the floor next to Charlie Bog and Polly Rickenbacker and across from Judy Pongarongatong.

"Banker!" shouted Willie Willies. "I get to be banker!"

"You can't play, Mr. Willies," said Polly Rickenbacker. "You cheat."

"I was just counting the money the last time," said Willies. "That's what bankers do. They count money."

"You weren-n-n-n't coun-n-nting-ng-ng mon-n-ney," said Judy Pongarongatong. "You were taking-ng-ng-ng mon-n-n-ney."

"Oh, so what," said Willies. "Some bankers do that, too." Then he went over into a corner and sulked.

Charlie started setting up the game, counting

out the money and putting the Chance and Community Chest cards on the board. Every once in a while when his antennae twitched, they would brush my face. It tickled like crazy.

"Sorry," Charlie would say. "Can-n-n't . . . can-n-n't help it."

We each chose a marker. Charlie chose the ship. Polly Rickenbacker chose the dog, and Judy Pongarongatong chose the cannon. I was glad that nobody wanted to be the hat. I always like to be the hat.

Every once in a while, as I watched Charlie and Polly and Judy take their turns, I would think, *Here I am, turning into a bug and playing Monopoly with three other kids who are turning into bugs in Edna Edge's old office at the Roseville Home for Lost Children.* But then it would be my turn and I would pass Go or land on a property or something, and I would stop thinking anything at all and just play the game.

While we played, Charlie Bog told me why he had eaten at Gussy's seventy-seven times in a row.

"I waz-z-z trying-ng to get famouz-z-z," he said. "So I could go on-n-n talk showz-z-z and everything-ng-ng. "

As it turns out, Charlie Bog loved talk shows. He got to see lots of them, too, because he was homeschooled and his mother usually just told him to watch a talk show and then do a report on it.

"I waz-z-z watching-ng-ng thoz-z-ze people on talk showz-z-z every day," Charlie said. "And then-n-n I thought, Why should-n-n-n't *I* get to be on-n-n a talk show?"

So Charlie got the idea that he would get to go on a talk show if he broke some kind of record or something. The trouble was, according to him, he wasn't that good at anything like sports or school or chess. This was just about the time that

Gussy's came to town. Somehow Charlie decided that if he could be the first kid to eat at Gussy's a thousand times in a row, he could go on a talk show and talk about it.

"The trouble iz-z-z," he said, "I turn-n-ned into a bug at seven-n-n-nty-seven-n-n."

The weird thing is when I asked Charlie Bog why he wanted to be so famous and be on a talk show, he didn't really know. His antennae twitched and he said, "I just do. That's all." That made me think that I am never going to do anything unless I know why I am doing it.

Judy Pongarongatong landed on Park Place and bought it. When she was counting out her money to pay for it, she said *she* had eaten at Gussy's so many times because she was collecting Gussy Trading Cards. She said that until she found out Gussy's was turning her into a bug, she thought Gussy Trading Cards were just about the coolest things in the world. She had something like two hundred and eighty of them. I decided not to tell her that Gussy was really a seventy-four-year-old lady.

Polly Rickenbacker got sent to Jail and swore up and down that she had never eaten at Gussy's and never would.

"Oh sure," said Willie Willies. "I guess you just naturally look like a bug."

That made Polly really mad. Who could blame her? She was about to say something back to Willies, but we never got to find out what it was because the door to Edna Edge's office suddenly swung open.

"Roscoe!" shouted my mother. "What on earth are *you* doing here? And who are these horrid-looking children?"

Chapter 15

ONE THING I have noticed is that almost every parent thinks that his or her kid is really cute even if the kid is really weird looking and everybody else thinks the kid is ugly. I noticed that because my mother thought the other three kids were horrid looking. But the truth is that I looked just as horrid as they did, or almost as horrid, and she didn't think I was horrid looking. Or if she did she didn't say that.

The other thing is that I really didn't think Charlie Bog looked that bad. In fact, his antennae looked kind of cool. At least *I* thought they did, the way he kept moving them around and every-thing.

Anyway, my mother had come out to the Roseville Home for Lost Children to take pic-tures for the report she was working on to change it into an orphan's museum. She hadn't known we were there or anything. She thought I was doing some anthropological work with Kinchy, so it was kind of an accident that she found us. Except when I think about it, it doesn't exactly seem like it was an accident, which gives me a really funny feeling.

Naturally, I was very surprised to see my mother but not as surprised as Willie Willies, who was kind of the nervous type, anyway, and who jumped straight up in the air when the door opened and my mother walked in.

It looked like a cartoon because when he jumped in the air, he started moving his legs like he was running. When he hit the floor, he was almost already out of the room. It didn't make any difference, though, because he ran right into the arms of the chief of police, who was walking into the Roseville Home for Lost Children at that very minute.

Kinchy told me later that after Willie Willies had grabbed me and put me into the bag at Gussy's, all kinds of things had happened. Cecil Geed had tried to run away, but Agnes Bean caught him before he even got out of the parking lot although she is twice as old as he is, which just goes to show you what a seventy-four-year-old lady can do if she has studied jujitsu long enough.

Kinchy said that Geed had cried like a baby and that he had even tried to bribe Agnes Bean by offering her a raise of two dollars a week. He even offered to let her honk the horn of his brand-new red cars instead of just listening to him do it.

While Agnes was catching Cecil Geed and threatening to do all kinds of jujitsu on him, Kinchy had run to the telephone and called the police.

It didn't take long for Cecil Geed to confess and tell them all about the giant bugs and the lot and everything. (Later the mayor tried to say he wasn't the one who had appeared in the *Roseville Recorder* with Cecil Geed and that it was just someone who looked like him and whose name he couldn't recall.)

But I still haven't told you the most amazing thing. The most amazing thing is that when my mother walked into Edna Edge's office and Willie Willies took off, he had just enough time to grab the door and pull it shut behind him. In fact, he pulled it so hard that the glass fell out of the door and shattered into a million pieces so that there was broken glass all over the place.

The pieces with Edna Edge's name on them fell right down by my feet. EDNA was all together but EDGE had broken into four separate pieces, with one letter on each. I couldn't believe my eyes! The pieces had scattered a little bit when they fell, so that instead of *E-D-G-E*, they now read *G-E-E-D*!

Yes! Cecil Geed, owner and president of Gussy's restaurants, was none other than Edna Edge's nephew, Sherman! Once he had grown up and left Roseville, he had changed his name because before he had the idea for Gussy's, he had gotten into trouble for kidnapping puppies and turning them into hot dogs. When he got the idea for Gussy's, he knew no one would buy Jungle Drums from a hot-dog-making pet-napper, so he changed his name from Sherman Edge to Cecil Geed.

No one knows why he ended up moving the Gussy's corporate headquarters back to Roseville. My mother said he wanted to lord it over all the orphans who still lived here, but I thought that wasn't right because they didn't know it was Edna Edge's nephew, Sherman. They thought he was Cecil Geed. But Kinchy said that that showed just how bad he really was. He didn't even need the orphans to know who he was! He liked to lord it over them in secret, and that gave me a really creepy feeling. I don't know why.

Anyway, Cecil Geed and Willie Willies ended up in the Roseville County Jail. Charlie Bog and Judy Pongarongatong even visited them a couple of times. They took their Monopoly game, and the four of them would play through the bars, but they finally stopped going because Willie Willies always cheated and Cecil Geed was always in a bad mood.

Some people are like that, I guess.

Chapter 16

WELL, NOW YOU KNOW everything, or almost everything. I think Kinchy was right. It *was* a good idea to write it all down, even though it was kind of hard. Kinchy hasn't read this yet. I wonder what she'll say.

Anyway, as it turned out, the bug process has reversed itself, just like Dr. Tristan VanNutz from the Institute for Science Gone Bad said it would. But it took some time, and it got worse before it got better. I even started to grow my own set of antennae! But they eventually began to shrink, and after about two months, I'm starting to get back to my old self. I still think my eyes are bigger now than they were before I got changed into a bug, but everybody says they look just the same. I don't know if they're telling the truth, though.

Charlie Bog got his wish. He really did get to be famous. But not because he had eaten at Gussy's a thousand times. It was because of his antennae! He even got to be on talk shows. But he told me later it wasn't nearly as much fun as he'd thought it was going to be, and that mostly people just called him names. After Charlie's antennae fell off, he tried to save them in a box under his bed, but after a week or so they just turned to dust. I felt kind of sorry about that. He really did look good in those antennae. Charlie goes to Roseville Elementary now.

Judy Pongarongatong threw away all her Gussy Trading Cards and she is now collecting Winkee Dolls. She has over seventy-five already!

As for Polly Rickenbacker, guess what? She

was telling the truth. She never had eaten at Gussy's. I knew that anybody who stamped her foot like that couldn't be telling a lie. As it turns out I never had seen her at Gussy's and it was just my active imagination that made me think I had. The sad thing is that Willie Willies was right. Polly Rickenbacker was just naturally starting to look like a bug. Polly's mother told her not to worry and said Polly was just going through an awkward stage. I guess that's possible, but Polly's mother kind of looks like a bug, too.

My mother was able to reopen the Roseville Home for Lost Children, but it's not called that anymore. Now it's called the Roseville Home for *Found* Children, which I think is a much better name. It's all painted and cleaned up — white with green shutters on every window. There's a big garden in front, too, with all kinds of flowers and everything, but it's not a museum.

Kids go there and stay for a while. I'm not sure why, but Kinchy says it's because those kids have been *traumatized*, which sounds a little bit like *transmogrified* but doesn't mean the same thing at all.

My mother made sure all the chairs at the Roseville Home for Found Children are big comfy ones. Wooden stools are not even allowed. Sometimes Kinchy and I ride our bikes out to the Roseville Home for Found Children and play with the kids.

Oh, there's one other thing about my mother. She almost never makes tuna surprise anymore. Last night we had couscous.

As for my father, well, his nerves are still shot, but he has applied for a new job in the cymbal *polishing* department, which he says is a much quieter job. I hope he gets it.

The biggest surprise is that Kinchy now says

she doesn't want to be an anthropologist. She says she is going to be an entomologist, which is a person who studies bugs. She says that from the minute she saw that giant bug on the meat grinder, she knew she wanted to know everything about it. I think that's really weird, but I'm not a certified genius. When I asked her about black widow spiders, she said entomologists only study bugs with six legs. Then she changed the subject.

Agnes Bean did go on safari, and she got kind of famous in Africa because she caught two poachers by pretending she was a gorilla. There was an article about her in the *Roseville Recorder*, with a picture of her doing a jujitsu move on the poachers, who looked really embarrassed.

In the article, Agnes Bean said something that I thought was very interesting. "Well," she said, "at least I have one thing to thank Cecil Geed for. If he hadn't made me dress up like Gussy all those years, I never would have known how to pretend to be a gorilla and those poachers would be free today."

That made me think that maybe someday I would be able to do something I would never have been able to do if I hadn't been transmogrified. I mean, I don't know what it would be or anything, but it might be true.

I just got a post card from Agnes Bean. She's back in Africa. On the front is a picture of a herd of elephants walking single file, and it looks really cool because the sun is setting behind them and all you can see are the outlines of those elephants and the red, red sky behind them. On the back Agnes wrote, "Well, Roscoe, I guess everything has turned out fine."

And I guess it has. In a way, when you think about it, I guess it always does.